Why Mosquitoes Buzz in People's Ears

Dial Books for Young Readers
New York
a pied piper book ®

Why Mosquitoes Buzz in People's Ears

A West African Tale | retold by
Verna Aardema
pictures by Leo and Diane Dillon

Library of Congress Catalog Number: 74-2886
First Pied Piper Printing 1978
Printed in the U.S.A.
(b)
14 15
A Pied Piper Book is a registered trademark of
Dial Books for Young Readers
A Division of Penguin Books USA Inc.
®TM 1,163,686 and ®TM 1,054,312
WHY MOSQUITOES BUZZ IN PEOPLE'S EARS
is published in a hardcover edition by
Dial Books for Young Readers
375 Hudson Street
New York, New York 10014
ISBN 0-8037-6088-4

The art for this book was prepared in full color using watercolors
applied with an airbrush in both fine spray and spatter technique,
pastels rubbed on by hand, and india ink. The cut-out
effect was achieved by actually cutting the shapes out of vellum
and frisket masks at several different stages.

One morning a mosquito saw an iguana drinking at a waterhole. The mosquito said, "Iguana, you will never believe what I saw yesterday."

"Try me," said the iguana.

The mosquito said, "I saw a farmer digging yams that were almost as big as I am."

"What's a mosquito compared to a yam?" snapped the iguana grumpily. "I would rather be deaf than listen to such nonsense!" Then he stuck two sticks in his ears and went off, mek, mek, mek, mek, through the reeds.

The iguana was still grumbling to himself when he happened to pass by a python.

The big snake raised his head and said, "Good morning, Iguana."

The iguana did not answer but lumbered on, bobbing his head, badamin, badamin.

"Now, why won't he speak to me?" said the python to himself. "Iguana must be angry about something. I'm afraid he is plotting some mischief against me!" He began looking for somewhere to hide. The first likely place he found was a rabbit hole, and in it he went, wasawusu, wasawusu, wasawusu.

When the rabbit saw the big snake coming into her burrow, she was terrified. She scurried out through her back way and bounded, krik, krik, krik, across a clearing.

A crow saw the rabbit running for her life. He flew into the forest crying kaa, kaa, kaa! It was his duty to spread the alarm in case of danger.

A monkey heard the crow. He was sure that some dangerous beast was prowling near. He began screeching

and leaping kili wili through the trees to help warn the other animals.

As the monkey was crashing through the treetops, he happened to land on a dead limb. It broke and fell on an owl's nest, killing one of the owlets.

Mother Owl was not at home. For though she usually hunted only in the night, this morning she was still out searching for one more tidbit to satisfy her hungry babies. When she returned to the nest, she found one of them dead. Her other children told her that the monkey had killed it. All that day and all that night, she sat in her tree —so sad, so sad, so sad!

Now it was Mother Owl who woke the sun each day so that the dawn could come. But this time, when she should have hooted for the sun, she did not do it.

The night grew longer and longer. The animals of the forest knew it was lasting much too long. They feared that the sun would never come back.

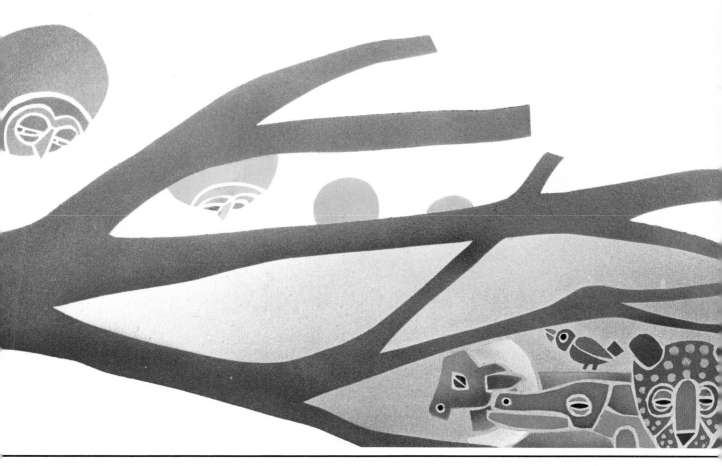

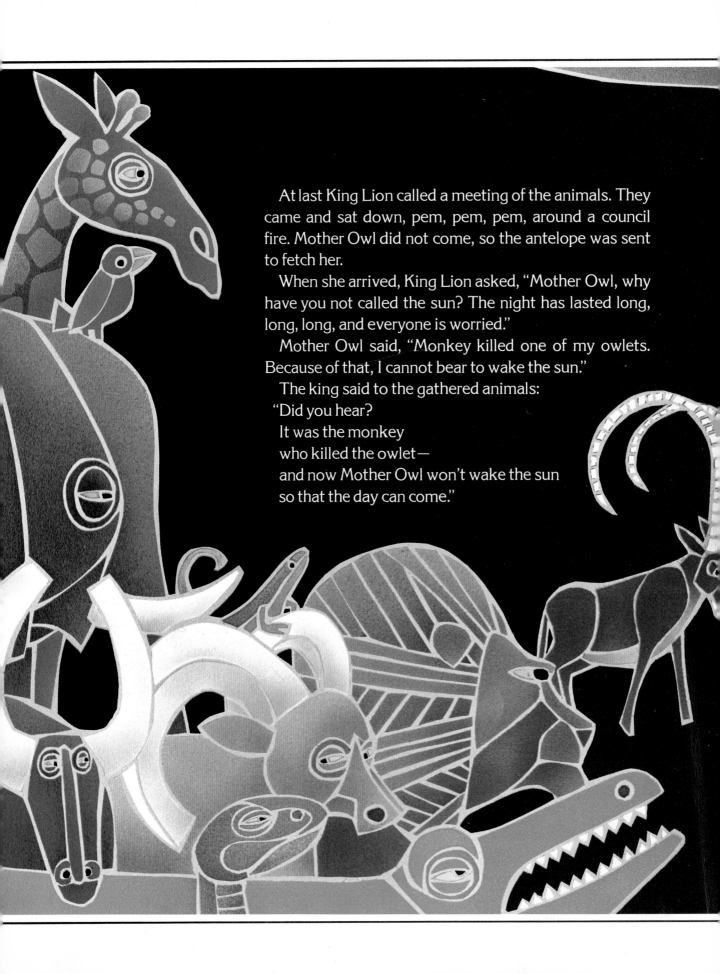

At last King Lion called a meeting of the animals. They came and sat down, pem, pem, pem, around a council fire. Mother Owl did not come, so the antelope was sent to fetch her.

When she arrived, King Lion asked, "Mother Owl, why have you not called the sun? The night has lasted long, long, long, and everyone is worried."

Mother Owl said, "Monkey killed one of my owlets. Because of that, I cannot bear to wake the sun."

The king said to the gathered animals:
"Did you hear?
It was the monkey
who killed the owlet—
and now Mother Owl won't wake the sun
so that the day can come."

Then King Lion called the monkey. He came before him nervously glancing from side to side, rim, rim, rim, rim.

"Monkey," said the king, "why did you kill one of Mother Owl's babies?"

"Oh, King," said the monkey, "it was the crow's fault. He was calling and calling to warn us of danger. And I went leaping through the trees to help. A limb broke under me, and it fell taaa on the owl's nest."

The king said to the council:

"So, it was the crow
who alarmed the monkey,
who killed the owlet—
and now Mother Owl won't wake the sun
so that the day can come."

Then the king called for the crow. That big bird came flapping up. He said, "King Lion, it was the rabbit's fault! I saw her running for her life in the daytime. Wasn't that reason enough to spread an alarm?"

The king nodded his head and said to the council:
"So, it was the rabbit
who startled the crow,
who alarmed the monkey,
who killed the owlet—
and now Mother Owl won't wake the sun
so that the day can come."

Then King Lion called the rabbit. The timid little creature stood before him, one trembling paw drawn up uncertainly.

"Rabbit," cried the king, "why did you break a law of nature and go running, running, running, in the daytime?"

"Oh, King," said the rabbit, "it was the python's fault. I was in my house minding my own business when that big snake came in and chased me out."

The king said to the council:
"So, it was the python
who scared the rabbit,
who startled the crow,
who alarmed the monkey,
who killed the owlet—
and now Mother Owl won't wake the sun
so that the day can come."

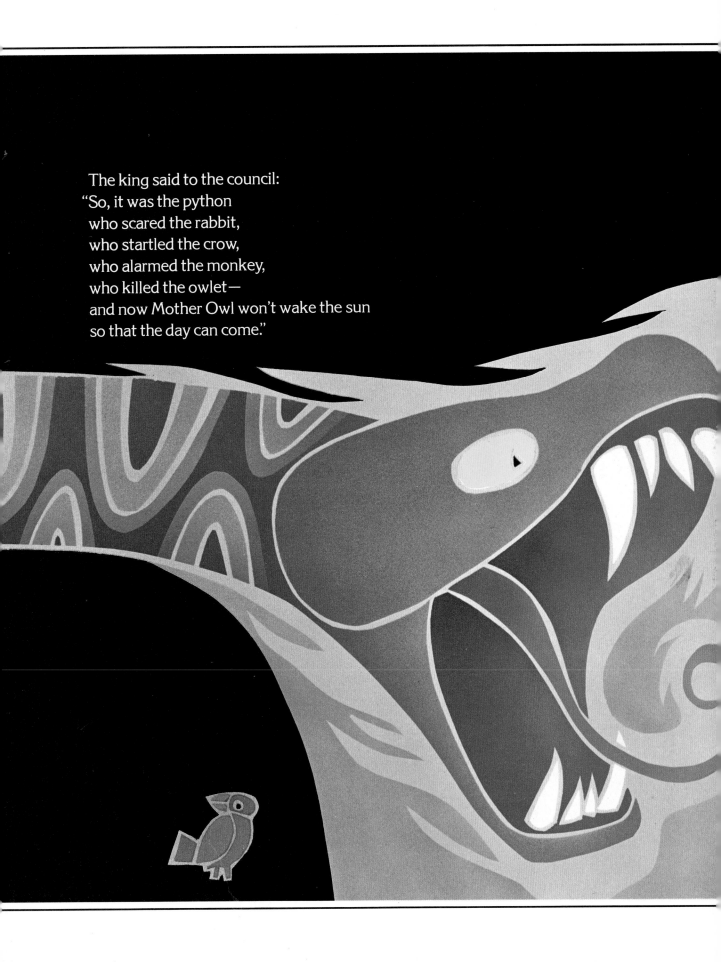

King Lion called the python, who came slithering, wasawusu, wasawusu, past the other animals. "But, King," he cried, "it was the iguana's fault! He wouldn't speak to me. And I thought he was plotting some mischief against me. When I crawled into the rabbit's hole, I was only trying to hide."

The king said to the council:
"So, it was the iguana
    who frightened the python,
    who scared the rabbit,
    who startled the crow,
    who alarmed the monkey,
    who killed the owlet—
and now Mother Owl won't wake the sun
so that the day can come."

Now the iguana was not at the meeting. For he had not heard the summons.

The antelope was sent to fetch him.

All the animals laughed when they saw the iguana coming, badamin, badamin, with the sticks still stuck in his ears!

King Lion pulled out the sticks, purup, purup. Then he asked, "Iguana, what evil have you been plotting against the python?"

"None! None at all!" cried the iguana. "Python is my friend!"

"Then why wouldn't you say good morning to me?" demanded the snake.

"I didn't hear you, or even see you!" said the iguana. "Mosquito told me such a big lie, I couldn't bear to listen to it. So I put sticks in my ears."

"Nge, nge, nge," laughed the lion. "So that's why you had sticks in your ears!"

"Yes," said the iguana. "It was the mosquito's fault."

King Lion said to the council:

"So, it was the mosquito
  who annoyed the iguana,
  who frightened the python,
  who scared the rabbit,
  who startled the crow,
  who alarmed the monkey,
  who killed the owlet —
  and now Mother Owl won't wake the sun
  so that the day can come."

"Punish the mosquito! Punish the mosquito!" cried all the animals.

When Mother Owl heard that, she was satisfied. She

turned her head toward the east and hooted: "Hoo!
Hooooo! Hooooooo!"
     And the sun came up.

Meanwhile the mosquito had listened to it all from a nearby bush. She crept under a curly leaf, *semm,* and was never found and brought before the council.

But because of this the mosquito has a guilty conscience. To this day she goes about whining in people's ears: "Zeee! Is everyone still angry at me?"

When she does that, she gets an honest answer.